AMAZING RACING CARS

DRAGSTERS

BY ASHLEY GISH

CREATIVE EDUCATION • CREATIVE PAPERBACKS

Published by Creative Education and Creative Paperbacks
P.O. Box 227, Mankato, Minnesota 56002
Creative Education and Creative Paperbacks are imprints of
The Creative Company
www.thecreativecompany.us

Design by The Design Lab
Production by Joe Kahnke
Art direction by Rita Marshall
Printed in China

Photographs by Alamy (Ian Shipley SP, Will Lester/ZUMA Wire, Jacob Paulsen/Southcreek Global/ZUMApress.com, Screenbyte, The Bakersfield Californian/ZUMAPRESS.com, Tony Watson, Dan Wozniak/Southcreek Global/ZUMAPRESS.com), Dreamstime (Steve Mann), Getty Images (Pat Brollier/The Enthusiast Network, Leo Mason/Popperfoto, Michael Reaves/The Denver Post), Newscom (David John Griffin/Icon Sportswire), Shutterstock (Gino Santa Maria, Michael Stokes, Vdant85)

Library of Congress Cataloging-in-Publication Data
Names: Gish, Ashley, author.
Title: Dragsters / Ashley Gish.
Series: Amazing racing cars.
Includes bibliographical references and index.
Summary: A fast-paced, high-interest introduction to dragsters, lightweight race cars known for their wide rear tires and use in drag races. Also included is a biographical story about dragster driver Antron Brown.
Identifiers: LCCN 2019049499
ISBN 978-1-64026-286-7 (hardcover)
ISBN 978-1-62832-818-9 (pbk)
ISBN 978-1-64000-416-0 (eBook)
Subjects: LCSH: Dragsters—Juvenile literature.
Classification: LCC TL236.2.G57 2021 / DDC 629.228/5—dc23

CCSS: RI.1.1, 2, 4, 5, 6, 7; RI.2.2, 5, 6, 7, 10; RI.3.1, 5, 7, 8; RF.1.1, 3, 4; RF.2.3, 4

First Edition HC 9 8 7 6 5 4 3 2 1
First Edition PBK 9 8 7 6 5 4 3 2 1

Table of Contents

Dragsters are speedy race cars. The first drag races happened in the 1930s. People sped across dry lakebeds in California. Later, drivers raced on empty runways and back roads.

In the 1960s, race cars went from wide and short to long and thin.

MONDELLO &
MATSUBARA
389 A/A
CHAMPION

PRO
43
SS

Dragsters are cars built to race on short tracks. Two common types of dragsters are top fuel and funny cars. Top fuel dragsters are long and lightweight. Funny cars are narrow and smooth.

Some cars shoot out nitrous gas to clear the lines before a race.

Also called floppers, funny cars shake and wobble more than other cars.

Many are made mostly of steel. But funny cars also have an outer body made of lightweight **carbon fiber**. This piece must be lifted to allow the driver to enter the car.

carbon fiber a strong, woven material

GOODRIDGE
LUCAS
OIL PRODUCTS INC.
CHAOS
ALAN JOHNSON
RCD
EAGLE
GOODYEAR

DRAGSTER JEFF
BEDROCK RACING
KERN
TRANSMISSION
CSI
RACING DIVISION

Dragster tires, called slicks, are soft and smooth.

Top fuel cars weigh at least 2,320 pounds (1,052 kg). They are about 25 feet (7.6 m) long. Their wide rear tires increase **traction** and improve **acceleration**. These cars can zoom faster than 335 miles (539 km) per hour.

acceleration increasing speed within a short time

traction the grip of a tire on the ground

Drag races usually involve two cars. Common drag race lengths are 1,000 feet (305 m) and a quarter mile (402 m). Each race, called a pass, lasts only a few seconds.

Racers who take off before the green light are disqualified.

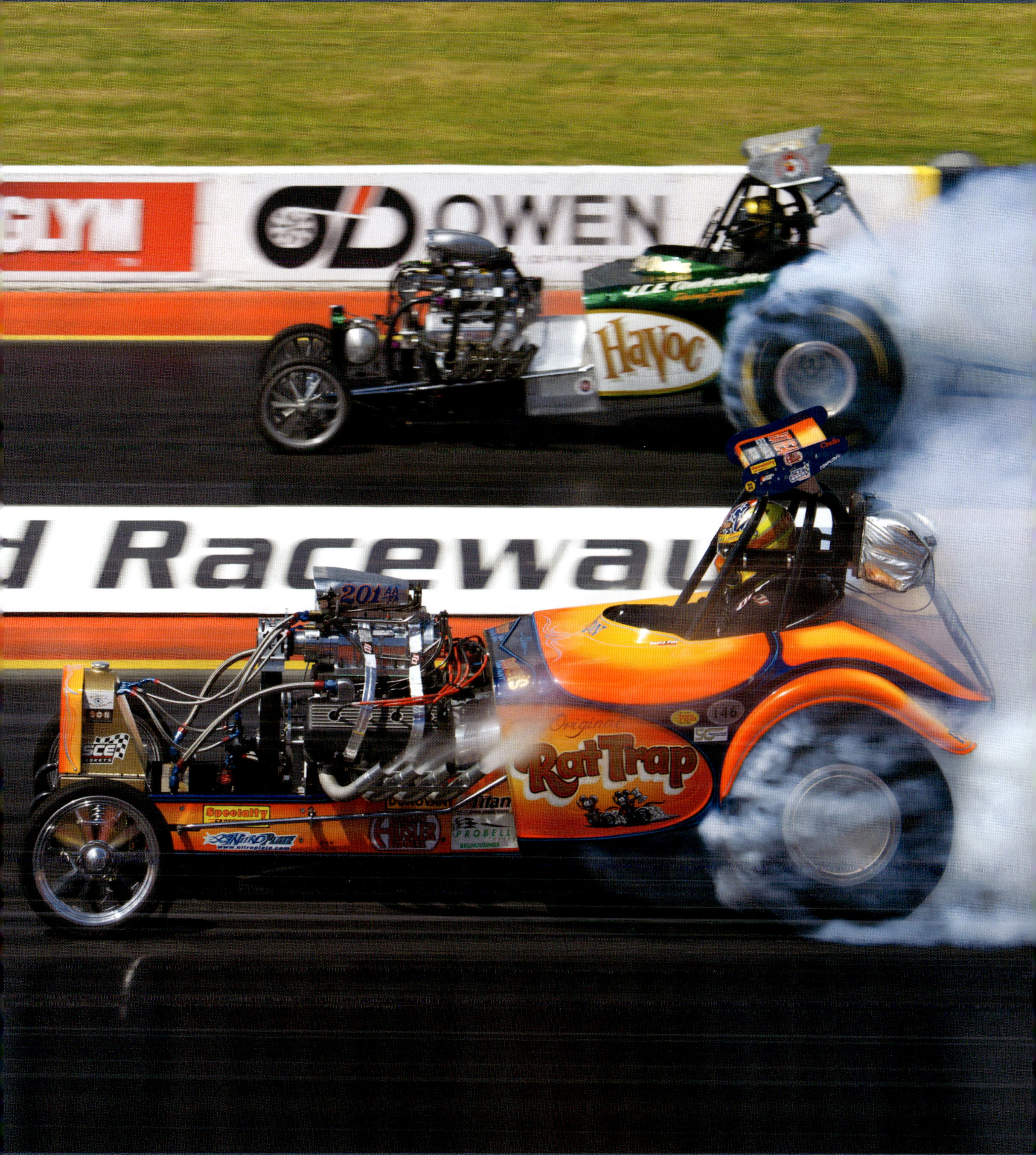
OWEN
Havoc
Rat Trap
Specialty

SANDVIK
Coromant
CHARGER
@MattHagan_FC
MOPAR
SANDVIK
Coromant
MOPAR
MOPAR.COM
PENNZOIL
PENNZOIL

The fastest dragsters use both brakes and parachutes to stop.

Drivers warm up dragster tires with a burnout. They accelerate suddenly. This causes the tires to spin, but the car does not move forward. Burnouts help the tires grip the track during the race. Then drivers pull up to the starting line. They wait for the green light to go. To slow down after a pass, racers release **parachutes**.

parachutes pieces of cloth that fill with air and act as a brake

Drivers wear flame-resistant bodysuits for safety.

Dragsters use a mix of **nitromethane** and **methanol**. This fuel gives the dragster more power. When nitromethane leaves the car's **exhaust** pipes, it mixes with air and creates flames.

exhaust the waste gases of a vehicle's engine

methanol a toxic, flammable liquid

nitromethane an oily liquid used as rocket fuel

CAMARO
AAA
SOUTHERN CALIFORNIA
Insurance
AUTO CLUB
DEWALT
AAA.com

In 2017, a funny car became the fastest dragster in history. Robert Hight sped down a quarter-mile track at more than 339 miles (546 km) per hour!

Robert Hight (above) was the National Hot Rod Association Funny Car champion in 2009 and 2017.

Dragsters are the fastest cars in the world. Clouds of smoke curl up from wide tires. Drivers tear down the short track. Flames burst from exhaust pipes.

A dragster engine can burn about one gallon (3.8 l) of nitromethane per second.

EAGLE RACING
MOTORSPORT

Driver Spotlight: Antron Brown

Antron Brown was just six years old when he started working on dragsters. He raced motorcycles in high school. In 2008, he started racing top fuel dragsters. Four years later, Antron became the first African American to win the National Hot Rod Association Top Fuel World Championship. He was also the first top fuel driver to finish a pass in under 3.7 seconds. Antron won two more world championships in 2015 and 2016.

MATCO TOOLS
MATCO TOOLS
Valvoline
U.S. ARMY
ARMY STRONG.
MATCO TOOLS
MATCO TOOLS

Read More

Adamson, Thomas K. *Dragsters*. Minneapolis: Bellwether Media, 2019.

Caswell, Deanna. *Funny Cars*. North Mankato, Minn.: Black Rabbit Books, 2018.

Fishman, Jon M. *Cool Drag Racing Cars*. Minneapolis: Lerner, 2019.

Websites

Kiddle: Auto Racing Facts for Kids
https://kids.kiddle.co/Auto_racing
Read more about dragsters and other race cars.

Science Trek: Force and Motion
https://sciencetrek.org/sciencetrek/topics/force_and_motion/
Explore this site to learn about force and motion.

SICK Science: Drag Racing Cups
https://www.stevespanglerscience.com/lab/experiments/drag-racing-coffee-cups/
Learn about energy and speed in this fun science experiment!

Note: Every effort has been made to ensure that the websites listed above are suitable for children, that they have educational value, and that they contain no inappropriate material. However, because of the nature of the Internet, it is impossible to guarantee that these sites will remain active indefinitely or that their contents will not be altered.

Index